Hang in there, Oscar Martin!

DIANA NOONAN

illustrated by Craig Smith

Learning Media

Chapter 1

Things weren't good at the office of the *Redmond School News*. The team gathered round the desk of Bobbie, the chief editor. "The paper's just not selling. No one in town wants to read it," she said.

"What about Mrs. Cortes?" asked Oscar. "I saw her take away a bunch of papers on Friday."

"She runs dog kennels, Oscar. She's lining them with the *Redmond School News* as we speak." Bobbie leaned across the desk. "Listen, Oscar, you're our best reporter."

"I'm your *only* reporter," he said.

"Exactly, and if you don't come up with a good story, nobody will. You've got two weeks to improve, or you'll lose your job. We'll all lose our jobs!"

Oscar gulped. "I may not be the best reporter in the world," he said, "but I'm not *that bad.*"

"Really?" asked Bobbie. "Take a look at this." She spread out the previous week's *Redmond School News* and pointed to the headlines.

"*Big Breakout – Four on the Loose,*" read Oscar. "That sounds exciting to me."

"Oh, yeah?" said Delwyn. "Let me read on." She leaned over the newspaper. "*There is little hope of finding alive the four who slipped between their bars on Friday night. The big worry is that they may break into gardens around the city. They are dangerous and should not be approached. A local pet shop owner describes the four as being gray and slimy, with light brown shells,*" she read. "We can't print any more snail stories, Oscar."

"It's not just your stories." Bobbie turned the page. "Your pictures are going to have to get better, too."

"What's wrong with that one?" asked Oscar, pointing. "It's a picture of our principal, Miss Davies."

"*You* know it's Miss Davies," said Bobbie. "*I* know it's Miss Davies. But no one else does. When you take someone's picture, you should always include their head."

"But everyone knows Miss Davies looks a lot better when you can't see her face," said Oscar.

"That's not good enough," said Bobbie. "Westbrook Elementary has just started up its own paper. It's called *Way Out West*."

"Yeah!" said Danny. "We have to be a whole lot better than them, or we'll be out of business."

Delwyn reached into her schoolbag. "Here's the camera, Oscar. And here's a notebook. Go to it! Give us a story that everyone will want to read."

Chapter 2

Every good reporter knows that if you want to get the best story and the best pictures, you have to be in the right place at the right time. That afternoon, Oscar took the long way home.

He went past the shops. Mr. Parker was standing outside his fruit and vegetable shop with a huge knife in his hand. He was hacking the outside leaves off his cabbages.

At the same time, a bus pulled up at the stop outside his shop, and a bunch of kids came running to catch it. Oscar knew a great story when he saw one. He waved his camera. "Hold it right there!" he called. "I'm from the news."

"The news?" Mr. Parker grinned. "I'm gonna be famous!" He held the knife high above his head. "How do I look?" he asked.

"Great," said Oscar. *Click*!

Oscar took out his notebook. "Children Run as Greengrocer Waves Knife ...." It sounded scary. With a headline like that, everyone would want to buy the paper.

"All I need now," thought Oscar, "is another story like that one."

He got his next lucky break as he was passing Webber's Toy City. Mrs. Webber was standing in the shop window. She was spreading out something big and yellow on the floor. Oscar went inside to check it out.

"Stand back," said Mrs. Webber. "This thing is going to blow up."

Oscar grabbed his camera.

Mrs. Webber switched on a machine that sounded like a vacuum cleaner. The yellow plastic began to grow.

"Do you like it?" asked Mrs. Webber when it had almost reached the roof. "It's an inflatable playhouse."

Click! "Downtown House Blows Up," wrote Oscar. "Thanks, Mrs. Webber. I just love it!"

Chapter 3

Across the road from Webber's, a window cleaner was working on the second floor of the Star Sky Tower. Someone who worked that high off the ground just had to know everything that was going on down below. Oscar decided to interview him.

"Can I come up?" called Oscar. "I'm from the news."

"Hey!" called the cleaner. "I'm gonna be in the paper! I'll be right down."

The cleaner was called Rob, and lucky for Oscar, he was very friendly. "Ask me anything you want," he said. "Only I have to keep working while I talk, so hop on."

Oscar hadn't been in a window cleaner's box before. It wobbled when he climbed in. Rob pressed a button, and the box rose up.

"W-what I really want to know," said Oscar, trying not to look down, "is … is … how safe is this thing we're standing in, anyway?"

"It's all very safe," said Rob. "Everything runs on electricity. I press this button here, and we go up. I press this one, and we go down."

The box dropped with a bump. Oscar's stomach did a flip. "Don't do that!" he said. The box began to climb again. The ground was getting further away by the minute. Oscar decided that the safest place was on the floor of the box. He crouched down and tried not to think about how far off the ground he was.

A few minutes later, the box stopped. Rob took his window cloth out of his back pocket. "This is the tallest building in town," he said. He stretched way out of the box and started washing a window. "How'd you like a picture of me cleaning the windows on the seventy-fifth floor?"

"Did you say … *seventy-fifth*?" whispered Oscar. He was too scared to move.

"That's right," said Rob. He leaned a little bit further out of the box. "Tell me when to say cheese."

There was no way Oscar was going to stay up this high. Without standing up, he reached for the down button. The box rocked and bumped. At the same time, Rob made a really tricky move. Suddenly he was hanging over the edge of the box by his ankles and screaming at the top of his voice.

"Boy!" said Oscar. "Some people will do anything to get their picture in the paper." He took a shot of Rob's ankles. *Click*!

By the time they'd reached the second floor of the Star Sky Tower, Rob was back in the box.

"I never knew window cleaning was so skilled," said Oscar. "Now, if I can just ask you a few questions ...."

Rob gave a groan. He slid down onto the floor of the box and closed his eyes.

"OK. We can talk later," said Oscar.

It wasn't so scary looking down from the second floor of the Star Sky Tower. Oscar got some great views of the street. He picked up his camera and started clicking. He got a shot of a police car speeding down Parkway Drive.

He got another shot of a bunch of people standing around outside a building. They had their hands up in the air. Oscar waved, but they didn't wave back. He put his zoom lens on his camera and took a few closeups.

A whole roll of film later, Rob opened his eyes. "Do you feel like answering a few questions now?" asked Oscar.

"Questions?" Rob looked over the edge of the box. "Sorry. I must have dropped off to sleep. I had this terrible dream that I was at the very top of the Sky Tower. I was hanging from the edge of the cleaning box by my ankles."

"Really?" asked Oscar.

"Yeah. It's enough to put me off cleaning windows for ever."

Chapter 4

That night, Oscar started writing up his stories. On the way to school next morning, he picked up his pictures from the camera shop. There was no time to look at them, so he tucked them into his schoolbag and set out for the newspaper office. The moment he opened the door, he knew that something was wrong. The room was empty.

Oscar put down his bag. "Where is
everyone?" he called. "Here I am, your best
and only reporter, with some great stories,
and there's no one here to read them."

Suddenly he heard voices, and the news
team burst in through the door. Bobbie was
holding a newspaper. Everyone else was
looking over her shoulder.

"What's going on?" asked Oscar. "The
Redmond School News doesn't come out
until the end of the week."

"This isn't the *Redmond School News*," said Bobbie. "It's *Way Out West*."

"We were lucky to get a copy," said Delwyn. "They've just sold out."

"I can't believe it," said Bobbie. "This is their first newspaper, and look at their front-page story. It's brilliant."

"*Daylight Robbery at City Bank*," read Oscar. "How come I'm never around when banks are being robbed?"

"They still haven't got the robbers," said Delwyn. "It says here that they had their faces covered with stockings so that no one could recognize them."

Bobbie put the paper down. She looked
hard at Oscar. "So what have you got to
beat a story like that?" she asked.

"An inflatable castle, a crazy greengrocer,
and a story about a window cleaner," said
Oscar flatly. "OK, OK, I know I have to go."

"How about your pictures?" asked Delwyn. "Did you manage to include a few heads this time?"

Oscar opened his schoolbag. He took out the pictures. There was a good one of Mr. Parker, but you couldn't see the knife. Mrs. Webber looked like she was standing in front of a giant grapefruit.

"What are these?" asked Bobbie.

"They're Rob's ankles," explained Oscar. "They're hanging over the edge of a window-cleaning box."

They looked at the photos he'd taken with his zoom lens. "This one's of a bunch of people," he said.

"I can see that," said Bobbie. "What are they doing? They've all got their hands in the air."

Oscar peered at the sign on the building in the picture. "They're standing outside the City Bank."

"The City Bank!" gasped Delwyn. "Oscar, what time did you take these photos?"

"It was after school, at about four o'clock."

"There's more!" shouted Danny. "Look, here's a shot of someone running down the steps of the bank. They've got a stocking over their head. Hey, it's the bank robber! And here's the driver of the getaway car. No wonder everyone has their hands up, the driver's holding a gun."

"Wait! Hold everything." Bobbie was tapping her finger against the last picture in the pile. "Oscar, you've done it! We've got a story that will sell every last newspaper we print."

Everyone pressed their heads together to look at the photo.

"It's the robbers in their getaway car," said Delwyn.

"You can see their faces!" said Danny. "The driver's taken the stocking off her head. The guy in the back seat has done the same thing."

"Action!" said the chief editor of the *Redmond School News*. "Delwyn, you call the police. Danny, can you make sure the printer is ready to roll. We're putting out a special edition."

"What do I do?" asked Oscar.

"Open your notebook and get writing," said Bobbie.

"But I don't know anything about the robbery."

"Just write about what you saw," said Bobbie. "You usually do. And by the way, where were you when you took those pictures?"

"You wouldn't believe me if I told you," said Oscar.

Chapter 5

The News team had never worked so hard or so fast. At nine o'clock the next morning, the *Redmond School News* hit the streets. Soon everyone was reading the main story.

City Bank Robbery Solved!

Redmond reporter Oscar Martin yesterday braved the heights of the Star Sky Tower for a bird's-eye view of the City Bank robbery. Using his zoom lens, he caught the City Bank robbers on film as they fled from the bank. By looking closely at shots of the getaway car leaving the scene of the crime, police have identified the robbers.

"Now that we know who we are looking for, we hope to catch the criminals in a few days," said Police Chief Spencer. He praised the quick action of Redmond Elementary's ace reporter, who leapt into the Sky Tower's window-cleaning box and rode up the side of the building to cover the story.

"We've done it!" said Bobbie. "We've sold every copy of the paper." The *Redmond School News* team were having a party in their office.

"What about Mrs. Cortes?" asked Delwyn. "What can she use in her dog kennels?"

"I told her to check out the Westbrook newsroom," grinned Bobbie.

"Does this mean I still have a job?" asked Oscar.

"It means you've got another chance," said Bobbie. "All you have to do is come up with another great story – every week."

"And by the way," said Delwyn, "the police called this morning. One of our readers told them that they saw you in the window cleaner's box on the Star Sky Tower. They said you took those photos hanging from your ankles, seventy-five floors up."

"But ..." began Oscar.

"No buts," said Bobbie. "The police are going to give you a special award. It'll be the paper's next big story."

"Will it ever!" said Danny. "And I've got the perfect headline –

Hang in There, Oscar Martin."